SPOTLIGHT ON GLOBAL ISSUES

EDUCATION FOR ALL

Amanda Vink

ROSEN PUBLISHING

NEW YORK

Published in 2022 by The Rosen Publishing Group, Inc.
29 East 21st Street, New York, NY 10010

First Edition

Editor: Theresa Emminizer
Book Design: Michael Flynn

Photo Credits: Cover Stuart Fox/Getty Images; (series globe background) photastic/Shutterstock.com; p. 4 Klaus Vedfelt/DigitalVision/Getty Images; p. 5 https://commons.wikimedia.org/wiki/File:Eleanor_Roosevelt_UDHR.jpg; p. 6 Darryl Brooks/Shutterstock.com; p. 7 Bettmann/Getty Images; p. 9 Fotosearch/Archive Photos/Getty Images; p. 10 littlenySTOCK/Shutterstock.com; p. 11 Dietmar/Temps/Shutterstock.com; p. 13 anasalhajj/Shutterstock.com; p. 14 https://en.wikipedia.org/wiki/George_W._Bush#/media/File:George-W-Bush.jpeg; p. 15 https://en.wikipedia.org/wiki/Every_Student_Succeeds_Act#/media/File:President_Barack_Obama_signs_Every_Student_Succeeds_Act_(ESSA).jpg; pp. 16, 21, 28 Monkey Business Images/Shutterstock.com; p. 17 SOMKKU/Shutterstock.com; p. 19 (miners) Tom Stoddart/Getty Images; p. 19 (coltan ore) Nada B/Shutterstock.com; p. 23 Marla Aufmuth/Getty Images; p. 24 David Grossman/Alamy Stock Photo; p. 25 Katarzyna Uroda/Shutterstock.com; p. 27 JP Yim/Stringer/Getty Images; p. 28 Billion Photos/Shutterstock.com.

Library of Congress Cataloging-in-Publication Data

Names: Vink, Amanda, author.
Title: Education for all / Amanda Vink.
Description: New York : Rosen Publishing, [2022] | Series: Spotlight on global issues | Includes index. |
Identifiers: LCCN 2019057072 | ISBN 9781725323193 (paperback) | ISBN 9781725323223 (library binding) | ISBN 9781725323209 (6 pack)
Subjects: LCSH: Educational equalization--United States--Juvenile literature. | Education--United States--Juvenile literature. | Youth--Political activity--United States--Juvenile literature.
Classification: LCC LC213 .V56 2022 | DDC 379.2/6--dc23
LC record available at https://lccn.loc.gov/2019057072

Manufactured in the United States of America

CPSIA Compliance Information: Batch #CSR22. For further information contact Rosen Publishing, New York, New York at 1-800-237-9932.

CONTENTS

CHAPTER ONE

EDUCATION: A RIGHT

A good education can change a person's life by giving them the skills to critically engage with the world. Education gives a person tools to better their situation. It empowers people to act in their own best interest. Educated people tend to earn more financially over the course of their lives, while a lack of a quality education feeds into the cycle of poverty. Because of this, providing education is one way for nations around the world to end extreme poverty, or people living on U.S. $1.90 or less a day. When governments focus on providing education, it makes life better for their citizens.

Eleanor Roosevelt was the chair of the United Nations Rights Commission, which created the Universal Declaration of Human Rights. In this picture, she's holding the finished document.

According to the United Nations (UN), education is a human right. On December 10, 1948, the UN issued the Universal Declaration of Human Rights, a document written by legal and cultural representatives from around the world. It sets out fundamental human rights that should be universally protected. Universal fundamental human rights are inherent to everyone, regardless of nationality, sex, religion, or sexual orientation. Article 26 of the Universal Declaration of Human Rights reads: "Everyone has the right to education."

Unfortunately, not everyone in the world receives a good education. In places all around the world, education is hard to come by, especially for children. Roughly 264 million kids don't have access to quality education. This is one of the great social issues of our time. Many organizations and individuals are trying to make accessible education a reality, but there's still a lot to do.

Modern education is usually made up of mandatory, or required, government-funded programming. Today, children in developed countries go to school multiple days a week and learn from a curriculum that's been standardized. There are government systems meant to make sure all students learn enough to graduate with a diploma, which is a document saying they've reached a certain standard of education.

This system isn't very old. When the first European settlers came to North America, they created the beginnings of their own education system. The goal was to teach children religious values and literacy, or reading and writing, so they could read the Bible.

These bricks mark the location of the original Boston Latin School built in 1635. The school was later moved.

SECOND BOSTON LATIN SCHOOL, 1812

In 1635, the Boston Latin School opened. It's widely considered the first public school in America. Soon after, the Massachusetts Bay Colony created a law that required towns to provide education for children. In 1837, the state of Massachusetts created the first state board of education to create a structure for schools to follow so all students would learn similar lessons.

In later centuries, however, with the rise of agriculture and industry, many children had to work in order to help their families survive. Unless a child came from a well-off family, it was likely they worked with their parents on a farm, in a factory, or in other ways.

It wasn't until the 19th century that governments passed child labor laws in England and later in the United States. These laws made it illegal to hire children under certain ages and put limits on how much they could work.

The first education secretary of Massachusetts was Horace Mann. Mann believed that, in a perfect world, education was a great equalizer—it allowed people to succeed no matter what their background. This viewpoint goes hand in hand with the American dream, the idea that any citizen in America can do well if they work hard. History has shown us that the American dream can be problematic because not everyone has the same privileges. Some people are born into circumstances that offer them fewer opportunities in life. It's true, however, that having access to quality education helps all people.

Education spreads awareness of things happening in the world, both positive and negative. Educated people have the tools to ask critical questions about what's happening around them, and they often have the skills to make plans and take action. Education builds confidence. It helps people realize they can make a difference in the world.

People who have quality education often choose lifestyles that allow them to maintain better health over the course of their lives. People of higher education backgrounds are less likely to smoke and less likely to abuse alcohol. They can more often choose and afford better quality food. These people often go for health checks more regularly, so problems are less likely to become chronic.

Evidence shows that greater investments in education decrease the rate of poverty, create long-term health benefits, and create greater gender equality. One single extra year of schooling can increase a person's earnings by up to 10 percent over the course of their lifetime.

Born in 1796, Horace Mann worked to improve the education system as the first education secretary of Massachusetts.

CHAPTER TWO

NO ACCESS

Children around the world lack access to basic education for many reasons. However, the main cause comes down to inequalities in money and distribution of resources. Money and resources aren't spread evenly among people living around the world. Some people have a lot of money while others have very little.

The people who don't have money and resources are left struggling to provide food, shelter, and basic human necessities for themselves and their families. Living conditions are extremely different around the world. The global average income in 2017 was $15,469. In that same year, the average person in the Central African Republic made $661 while the average person in Qatar made $116,936. Even within these countries, there are some people who earn far more than others. In the United States, income inequality is growing. In 2015, the top 10 percent of households in America made an average of $312,536 while the bottom 90 percent averaged $34,074.

This school in Malawi looks quite different from the American school shown on the left.

Poverty has a big impact on education. Children who live in poor areas likely may not have access to the best schools. Poverty also affects how well a person learns. For example, not having enough to eat can affect the brain's ability to learn. In the United States, one in seven children live with hunger. Poverty can also create stressful home lives, which makes concentrating and completing homework difficult. In areas with high poverty rates, it's more likely that children drop out of school.

CHAPTER THREE

EDUCATION AROUND THE WORLD

In some areas of the world, violence and war affect people's everyday lives. In these areas, it can be dangerous to go to school. In Syria, which has been locked in a civil war, an estimated 2 million children aren't attending school. Over 7,000 Syrian schools are damaged or ruined, so children have nowhere to go to class. In other places, there aren't enough schools, and the ones available are too far away for children to make it every day.

Some people can't afford to send their children to school. This could be because the uniform and book costs are too high. Children sometimes need to work to make money for their families. Sometimes there is no teacher. There may not be money to hire a teacher or there may not be a qualified individual in the area. Some schools don't have electricity or running water.

Natural disasters and environmental problems can also get in the way of schooling. In some areas, technology can help overcome these difficulties. In Beijing, China, there are days of high pollution that make it hard for people to leave their homes. Teachers can broadcast their lessons to students, who can watch from smart devices in their homes.

Even in developed countries, access to full education isn't always available. Funding isn't always distributed equally. For example, some schools might have funding for new equipment for chemistry labs, while others may not even have a chemistry lab.

These students in Yemen are studying in a house because it's too dangerous to go to school.

Public school in the United States looks very different today than it did back when it was first created. The Elementary and Secondary Education Act (ESEA) was first signed in 1965 by President Lyndon Johnson. Its goal was to improve educational inequalities by providing federal funds to school districts with low-income students. The ESEA remains the largest source of spending on education.

The act has been reauthorized, or renewed, eight times. In 2001, President George W. Bush famously gave the piece of legislation a new name: No Child Left Behind. Standardized testing became the main focus. The idea was that schools must meet yearly goals that would eventually have all kids at their grade levels. Critics of No Child Left Behind argued that the rules were too strict for schools and they actually made it more difficult for struggling schools to help students.

GEORGE W. BUSH

In December 2015, President Barack Obama signed ESSA into law.

In 2015, the law was given a new name again: the Every Student Succeeds Act (ESSA). ESSA gave schools more flexibility—it focuses on students' academic growth and allows schools to replace the statewide standardized tests with other nationally recognized tests.

Despite all this legislation coming from the federal government, in matters of policy, it's state and local governments that make decisions about education. This was part of the 10th Amendment to the U.S. Constitution. Because of this, standards can be very uneven, and school districts with more money tend to devote more resources to their schools.

CHAPTER FOUR

CRITICISMS OF THE U.S. SCHOOL SYSTEM

Critics of the modern education system point out that education isn't the great equalizer that was once imagined. Besides the financial inequalities, there are several major issues with the American school system.

School curriculums don't reflect the experiences of all people. The accounts of history that are taught often leave out the voices of many underrepresented people. There have also been problems with cultural divides between teachers and their students. Critics argue that it would be helpful for students to learn from teachers with many different backgrounds, both similar and different from their own cultural experience.

People learn differently from one another. A lot of people argue that standardized testing isn't a fair measure of kids' abilities.

Schools also aren't created equal when it comes to specialized programming, such as advanced placement, vocational training, and special education. Children have different needs, and critics of the modern school system argue that the current system treats children as if they are all the same—and it encourages them to be the same.

Some people believe schools today are designed to discourage creative thinking. They argue that students are taught to memorize and do well on standardized tests, but unique ideas and nonconformity aren't valued. Children are hardwired to play, while most curricular activities force them to sit at a desk for long periods of time. Much of what kids learn in school is meant to prepare them for the job market. With more and more kids being encouraged to attend college in order to get any kind of job, there's an economic burden placed on many families as well.

CHAPTER FIVE

TECHNOLOGY AND EDUCATION

Having access to technology can support learning. Some new programs allow educators to work with students at each level. This is called adaptive learning software—and it's becoming easier to use this technology on a wider scale. As students work, technology gives the teacher real-time information about how much information each student understands. This allows the teacher to create a more personalized approach. Some artificial intelligence (AI) technology is being used to tutor students. In a rapidly changing learning environment, it remains to be seen how these technologies will be used in the future. Will all children have access, or just a lucky few in the most developed (and wealthy) countries?

It's important to note that technology doesn't necessarily replace the human element to learning. In fact, teachers will remain just as important as before. If used correctly, technology in the classroom should help teachers do their jobs better and help students learn in more effective ways. It's important to remember that technology is a tool, not a solution.

Another important thing to note is that new technologies don't come without a cost. Resources needed to make new technologies and keep them running are often very harmful to the planet. Technologies that use screens, such as computers and smart devices, are made using rare minerals that need to be mined from Earth. This process lets out a large amount of carbon, and it also forces people to work in dangerous conditions.

These children in the Democratic Republic of Congo are mining for coltan, a metallic ore that's used to make many electronics.

CHAPTER SIX

BEYOND ECONOMICS

Perhaps the most important thing for students and society to decide on is what students should be getting out of education.

There are many people who argue that education should just be job training. Without a good education, you can't get a good job or make something of yourself. People who argue this point may believe that formal education is time wasted—time that should be spent on vocational training or learning a trade in an apprenticeship. Vocational training and apprenticeships are very valuable. Our society needs people who know how to perform specific tasks. But getting an education isn't and shouldn't just be about jobs and economics.

When students have the time and space to become curious about and develop skills with which to interact with the world, that's the true gift of education. As human beings, we have social duties that go beyond ending up in a good job and providing for ourselves and our families. We have responsibilities to do our best to help people who need it, to make sure we're living in a fair society, and to make sure government officials aren't using their offices for personal gain.

Education helps us think about these issues. In fact, throughout history, dictatorships have made information more difficult to come by. In countries with overly controlling governments, newspapers are often censored, or suppressed, to only include information that's in line with the government's viewpoints.

Learning self-confidence and how to become an engaged citizen are extremely important.

CHAPTER SEVEN

FIGHTING FOR EDUCATION

The fight for education can have high costs. In 2012, 15-year-old Malala Yousafzai was shot in the head by a Taliban gunman because she'd spoken up in support of the right for girls to be educated. Malala was born in Swat, an area of Pakistan. Once, the area had been largely self-governing and had a good school system. After the United States–led invasion of Afghanistan, Taliban power rose with strong anti-Western feelings. It became dangerous for girls to attend school. In 2008, the Taliban leaders of Swat issued a warning—all education of girls was to stop.

Malala wrote an anonymous, or nameless, blog called *Diary of a Pakistani Schoolgirl* for the news outlet BBC Urdu. She also spoke out to a Pakistani television presenter. She became well known in the area. Malala was heading home from school that day in 2012 when two men stopped the bus. "Who is Malala?" one asked. Everyone looked to her—and the man shot her in the head.

Malala had surgery to save her life. She was moved to Great Britain to heal. Nine months after the shooting, Malala stood at the UN headquarters in New York and spoke to a youth gathering. In 2014, at age 17, she became the youngest person to receive the Nobel Peace Prize. Malala remains outspoken about education and about how everyone deserves the opportunity to learn in a safe environment. She's also spoken about how the fight for education forced her to leave her homeland.

Malala still speaks up for many people around the world. In 2019, her newest book, *We Are Displaced*, was published.

CHAPTER EIGHT

THE RIGHT TO MAKE CHANGE

Every day, normal kids choose to devote themselves to bigger issues. On November 18, 2019, dozens of students in New York City took part in a strike for integration. The strike was the first organized by Teens Take Charge, a student-led movement to demand educational equality in New York City. They planned to lead a new strike at a different school every week until things changed.

The striking students that first day came from two different schools that share a building. However, the two groups had very different experiences, racial makeup, resources, and curriculum. One protestor pointed out that although New York City is often cited as one of the most progressive cities in the world, it still has an incredibly segregated school system. In the New York City school system, fewer African American and Latinx students attend the city's top public high schools than white students. Students involved with Teens Take Charge have waited for changes from city officials but, tired of waiting, they've started protesting instead.

Students around the world create change by protesting in order to make their opinions known.

This is just one example of how a group of kids can work to change things. It's important for kids to know their rights so that they can participate and share their opinions. Every student in the United States has rights upheld by the Constitution. That means they have the right to free speech and to hand out flyers, as long as they don't get in the way of the school's workings. Sometimes, school administration will work with students when they want to participate in a walkout; other times, they won't.

Often, people believe that their voice can't make a difference—especially if they're too young to vote for elected officials. However, as many young activists have proved, one voice can make a huge difference.

Amanda Gorman is another young person who's used her voice to call for change. In 2017, when she was 19, Gorman became the first Youth Poet Laureate of the United States. Using this position, Gorman has spoken at the Library of Congress and other places. Before that, as Youth Poet Laureate of Los Angeles, she visited the White House to meet with First Lady Michelle Obama. Gorman is also founder and executive director of One Pen One Page, a literacy program that creates free creative writing programming for underserved youth.

Activists work to bring education to more children every day. You can help, too. This can start right in your own community. Literacy is a growing concern across the United States and the world. Of high school graduates, only 37 percent are at or above a level of reading proficiency. There are many ways you can help people in your community and encourage literacy rates.

- Get a library card. Not only will it allow you to borrow books, but each card issued helps determine how much financial funding the library receives.
- Organize a fundraiser to donate supplies to a classroom.
- Volunteer for your local literacy organization–or help create one.
- Organize a youth open mic event.
- Create a book club.
- Collect books for low-income areas.

Amanda Gorman says that she was inspired after watching a speech by Malala Yousafzai.

Before you can make your voice heard, it's important to gather information and decide on a course of action. Getting very specific about an issue and your feelings about it can often make all the difference to the success of your project.

What do you want your educational system to look like? It might be helpful to study educational systems from around the world and decide what you think works and doesn't work. For example, in Finland there are no standardized tests (except for one voluntary test) and teachers are required to have master's degrees. In the Netherlands, students can enter one of three different types of schools after graduating from primary school. Each type of school has a different focus, which gives students options about the kind of schooling they want to participate in. In some places around the world, students have different schedules than in the United States. For example, in Brazil, some students go to school from 7 a.m. to noon. Do any of these models appeal to you?

In some countries, most students wear uniforms to attend classes.

How can you help people at home and across the globe? Here are some ways you might think about keeping up to date on educational policy and where you fit in the system:

- Follow local politics and stay up to date on current events.
- Write a newspaper opinion piece.
- Write a letter to an elected government official.
- Engage with other students.
- Become a tutor.
- Start a petition, or a formal written request for change.

CHAPTER NINE

BEING INFORMED AND GETTING INVOLVED

Education is a fundamental human right. There's no question that all people should have access to the resources they need to gain knowledge and build skills for a successful future.

But what's the best way to provide quality education to everyone around the world? Differences in people's situations makes providing fair access to education very difficult. The financial and social situation we are born into is completely out of our individual control. Sometimes, no matter how hard a person works, it can't make up for the inequalities they have to fight to overcome. Still, there's a lot we can do.

Starting in December 2019, the COVID-19 pandemic rocked the world. The disease spread quickly through many areas, and people didn't know how to keep themselves safe. As the weeks and months went on, groups such as the World Health Organization (WHO) worked to spread awareness about the disease and how to protect yourself and others. While some people refused to follow the rules set forth by these groups, others embraced the guidelines, which included wearing masks and social distancing in public. Schools across the country worked to educate people about COVID-19 and to keep students safe. The spread of information surrounding COVID-19 helped keep people healthy.

Education can be a tool to improve the quality of life for many people—if we recognize and work around the inequalities of society. Bringing education to people around the world is possible, and it starts by becoming informed and involved.

GLOSSARY

academic (aa-kuh-DEH-mik) Connected with a school.

activist (AK-tih-vist) Someone who acts strongly in support of or against an issue.

apprenticeship (uh-PREN-tis-ship) A period in which a young person works with an experienced person to learn a skill or trade.

chronic (KRAH-nik) Continuing or occurring again and again for a long time.

curriculum (cuh-RIH-kyuh-luhm) All the courses of study offered by a school.

dictatorship (dik-TAY-tuhr-ship) A government run by one person or a small group with absolute power.

distribution (dih-struh-BYOO-shuhn) How something is divided and spread out.

document (DAH-kyoo-muhnt) A written or printed statement that gives official information about something.

inherent (in-HAIR-uhnt) Belonging to the basic nature of someone or something.

integration (in-tuh-GRAY-shuhn) The state of bringing different races, genders, or social classes together to form one group.

investment (in-VEST-muhnt) The act of putting out money or energy, often in order to make a profit.

nonconformity (nahn-kuhn-FOR-muh-tee) Failure or refusal to behave the way most people behave.

proficiency (pruh-FIH-shuhn-see) Being proficient, or skilled, at something.

progressive (pruh-GREH-sihv) Interested in new ideas, marked by progress.

segregated (SEH-grih-gay-tuhd) Set apart or separated from others, especially because of race.

standardized (STAN-duhr-dizd) Brought into conformity with a standard way.

Taliban (TAA-lih-ban) A fundamentalist Islamic militia in Afghanistan.

technology (tek-NAH-luh-jee) A method that uses science to solve problems and the tools used to solve those problems.

vocational (voh-KAY-shnuhl) Of, relating to, or undergoing training in a skill or trade to be pursued as a career.

voluntary (VAH-luhn-tayr-ee) Done, given, or acting of free choice.

INDEX

PRIMARY SOURCE LIST

Page 5
Eleanor Roosevelt holding poster of the Universal Declaration of Human Rights. Photograph. Lake Success, New York. November 1949. Obtained through Wikimedia Commons.

Page 7
The Old Latin School illustration. Sketch. Boston, Massachusetts. 1886. Held by Getty Images.

Page 9
Horace Mann. Photograph. Taken before 1859. Held by Getty Images.

WEBSITES

Due to the changing nature of Internet links, Rosen Publishing has developed an online list of websites related to the subject of this book. This site is updated regularly. Please use this link to access the list: www.powerkidslinks.com/SOGI/education